One Acts That Don't Suck Anthology
Vol. 1

Four short, one act plays
that aren't boring or stupid

by
Caroline Haroldson

PREMIERE

All four, <u>One Acts that Don't Suck</u> short plays included in this anthology premiered at the One Acts that Don't Suck Festival on August 19th, 2016 in the Lakeridge Black Box Theatre, Lake Oswego, OR.

<u>CLYDE'S CONSCIENCE</u>
Directed by Lily Gleason

Conscience	Yelena Friedman
Clyde	Jordan Clarke
Sarah	Carly Wood

<u>CHEAPER THAN THERAPY</u>
Directed by Caroline Haroldson and Elliott Wells

David	Elliott Wells
Jennifer	Caroline Haroldson

<u>HOW TO RUIN YOUR LIFE IN 15 MINUTES</u>
Directed by Lucas Friedman

Emily	Lily Gleason
Hannah	Yelena Friedman
Sam	Michael Fain

<u>THESE SEATS ARE TAKEN</u>
Directed by Michael Fain

Theodore	Elliott Wells
Charles	Jacob Skidmore

ABOUT THE AUTHOR

 Caroline Haroldson divides time between Boston MA, Portland OR, and London UK. Training includes RADA (Royal Academy of Dramatic Arts, London) short course and RSAC (Rutgers Summer Acting Conservatory). At the time of publication, she is pursuing a BFA at the Boston Conservatory at Berklee. She is the founder of the Lake Oswego Experiential Theatre Project which seeks to produce adapted and original works in unconventional settings. In addition to all things theatrical, Caroline likes sloths, plaid pants, and green juice.

Find her at:

 caroline_haroldson
OneActsThatDontSuck.com

#oneactsthatdontsuck

TO THE READER

You've likely found your way to this book while searching for a short scene to do for a drama class or one act event. You may have already poured through an overwhelming pile of scripts that are wrong for one or more reasons. Maybe they are too long, too short, have characters that are too young, too old, or dialog that sounds like your grandma wrote it.

What you want seems so simple, right? Characters that are your age. Easily arranged staging. A small number of characters. Short. Dialogue that sounds the way you actually speak. You'd also like to find a comedy that is actually funny.

The author knows your struggle all too well. As a high school Thespian, Caroline Haroldson spent hours searching for workable material for drama class and Thespian events. She eventually gave up and solved her own problem by writing them herself and for members of her Drama Club.

The first four are included in this anthology. She gives you her blessing to stage them, cast them, perform them as you wish. If you need a little inspiration, check out our YouTube channel One Acts that Don't Suck to see them performed. You will also find links on oneactsthatdontsuck.com and from the One Acts That Don't Suck Facebook page.

And please, upload videos of your performances. We'd love to see them.

- **One Acts that Don't Suck**

TABLE OF CONTENTS

<u>HOW TO RUIN YOUR LIFE IN 15 MINUTES</u>

A 15-minute One Act Play
for
2F, 1M

By
Caroline Haroldson

Cast of Characters

Emily: The youngest in
                                her family. Uses
                                her charm to get
                                out of trouble.

Hannah: Emily's
                                responsible older
                                sister.

Sam: Emily's boyfriend.
                                A wholesome teen-
                                age boy.

Props needed: Shoe box, sweater, two
frames, text book, misc. items found in a
messy bedroom.

Set requirements: Closet (could be
curtain).

Scene

Emily's bedroom. A typical teenager's
bedroom, but especially messy with clothes,
food wrappers, and school supplies
scattered around the room. A picture of her
with Hannah is visible in the room, as is a
photo of Sam.

Time

Present day.

AT RISE: EMILY is standing in the middle
of her messy bedroom.

                    EMILY
Hi. I'm Emily, and this is the story of how
I ruined my life in 15 minutes. That's my
sister, Hannah.
                    (Points to photograph of
                    HANNAH)
She's the most resourceful person I have
ever met. She can do no wrong. My polar
opposite and still, somehow, hands down my
favorite person. In 8 minutes and 42
seconds she will no longer trust me.
                    (References photograph of
                    SAM)
See him? That's Sam. Headed to Dartmouth in
September on a partial scholarship, a
literal genius in every sense of the word.
He's going to dump me in exactly 13 minutes
and 27 seconds. The worst part? I deserve
it. The icing on the cake is that in 14
minutes and 31 seconds, I will have done
something disgustingly awful, completely on
my own, and without the fault of anyone
else. Over there? My closet. You'll find
out about what's in there soon enough. The
fifteen minutes start... now.
                    (Clicks button on stopwatch.
                    Hannah enters.)

                    HANNAH
Whoa, what am I looking at here?
                    (EMILY is quiet)
Are you ok?

3

                    EMILY
No.

                    HANNAH
Anything I can do?

                    EMILY
No.

                    HANNAH
               (Playful)
I don't need to beat anyone up, do I?

                    EMILY
No.

                    HANNAH
Alright then.
               (Turns to go)
You know, you'd better clean this up before
Mom gets home unless you want her to pop a
blood vessel or something.

                    EMILY
Thanks.

                    HANNAH
I can help out if you want. I don't have
any plans until, like, 6:00.
                    (Starts to pick up clothes
                    off the floor and walks
                    towards the closet)
I don't know what's going on, but if you
just need to sit and cry, that's ok.

                    EMILY
No, really, it's okay. I got it.

                    HANNAH
I'm literally offering to clean your room
for you, don't be stupid.

                    (HANNAH walks towards
                    closet)

                    EMILY
                    (Bolts upright)
Don't do that.

                    HANNAH
Do what?

                    EMILY
Don't open the closet.

                    HANNAH
What? Why?

                    EMILY
Just trust me on this.

                    HANNAH
                    (Very seriously)
Emily, is there a dead body in there?

                    EMILY
Not...exactly.

                    HANNAH
WHAT THE HELL, EMILY?

                    EMILY
Okay, look, it's not as bad as it sounds...

                    HANNAH
Just tell me what's in your closet.

                    EMILY
I really don't want to tell you.

                    HANNAH
Do it anyway.

                    EMILY
Hannah, just leave it alone.

                    HANNAH
                    (Stands and stares for a
                    second)
Fine.
                    (Drops clothes)
Fine.
                    (Walks towards door but
                    stops)
Emily, is there a boy in there?

                    EMILY
Definitely not.

                    HANNAH
                    (Gasps)
There's a BOY in there.

                    EMILY
I literally just said there wasn't, would
you chill?

                    HANNAH
I don't believe you.

                    EMILY
Why not?

                    HANNAH
Oh please, you can practically SMELL the
hormones in here.

                    EMILY
That's disgusting.

                    HANNAH
You're disgusting, hiding a boy in the
closet.

                    EMILY
I'M NOT HIDING A BOY IN THE CLOSET.

                    HANNAH
So you wouldn't mind if I just..maybe...I
don't know...shouted one of your deepest,
darkest secrets?

                    EMILY
If it would make you feel better.

                    HANNAH
Okay.
          (Looks directly at EMILY)
Emily wore a diaper until she was seven
years old.
          (Silence)

                    EMILY
Was that good for you? Did you enjoy that?
          (Beat)
Can you go now?

                    HANNAH
I just don't understand what could possibly
be in that closet to be such a big deal.

7

                    EMILY
Nothing you need to concern yourself with.
So go.

                    HANNAH
Whatever.
                    (Leaves. Then runs back
                    onstage.)
Emily listens to Nickelback!
                    (HANNAH exits.)

                    EMILY
Stop it!
                    (Gets up and walks towards
                    closet, goes to open it but
                    stops)
Hannah?

                    HANNAH
                    (Offstage)
What?

                    EMILY
Come in here.

                    HANNAH
                    (Enters)
What.

                    EMILY
There's a squirrel in the closet.

                    HANNAH
WHAT?

                    EMILY
There's a squirrel. In the closet.

                    HANNAH
              (Stares for a beat)
You're kidding.

                    EMILY
I wish.

                    HANNAH
Dead or alive?

                    EMILY
I don't know.

                    HANNAH
Wait. What??

                    EMILY
Ok, it's a long story.

                    HANNAH
I don't care. I want to hear it.

                    EMILY
Ok fine. I was driving home from school and
I wasn't paying attention and I kind of hit
a squirrel.

                    HANNAH
Kind of? How do you kind of hit a squirrel?

                    EMILY
Okay fine, I hit a squirrel. I definitely
hit a squirrel. Anyway, it wasn't dead, so
I took it home.

                    HANNAH
You took it WHERE?

                    EMILY
I thought I could help it! I don't know. It
was bleeding so I left it on the bed to go
get some paper towels to clean up.

                    HANNAH
Because that's smart.

                    EMILY
I didn't think that through. It wasn't
moving, I didn't think it could do much.

                    HANNAH
Makes sense.

                    EMILY
And when I came back it was gone and my
room was a mess.

                    HANNAH
Gone? Like disappeared?

                    EMILY
Well...

                    HANNAH
Oh jeez.

                    EMILY
I know, it's crazy.

                    HANNAH
Whatever. Just tell me how this thing ended
up in the closet.

                    EMILY
Well obviously I started looking for it.

HANNAH
Why didn't you call anyone?

EMILY
I don't know, I thought I had it covered.

HANNAH
Logical.

EMILY
Well, turns out it was under my bed.

HANNAH
Mhm...

EMILY
And it started running around making these
weird noises and hissing.

HANNAH
Maybe because it's RABID??

EMILY
I just wanted to put it out of its misery,
so I hit it a couple of times with this
textbook.

HANNAH
Wait, that calc book?

EMILY
Yep.

HANNAH
You're not talking calc.

                        EMILY
                     (Nervous)
Uh...no.

                        HANNAH
Why would you have a calc book when you're
not taking calc?

                        EMILY
I mean...I don't know...It was just there.

                        HANNAH
I'm taking calc.

                        EMILY
                     (Relieved)
Right.

                        HANNAH
Why do you have my calc book?

                        EMILY
I don't know...you probably left it here.
It was the first thing I grabbed.

                        HANNAH
Wait a minute, you KILLED a SQUIRREL with
my calc book??

                        EMILY
Not on purpose! Plus, there's a very real
possibility it could still be alive.

                    HANNAH
Let me get this straight; you hit a
squirrel with your car, took it home with
the intention of nursing it back to health,
where you then tried to kill it. AGAIN.
Then, threw it in a closet??

                    EMILY
                 (Silence)
Well, when you put it that way--

                    HANNAH
What were you thinking? There is so much
that is messed up about that. Emily, this
is the WORST mess you have ever gotten
yourself into.

                    EMILY
I mean...

                    HANNAH
It's like your life is just a montage of
poorly made decisions. Do you ever think
things through? Do you think consequences
just don't apply to you? What is it?

                    EMILY
Are you going to help me deal with it or
not?
                    (There is a thump in the
                    closet)

13

                    HANNAH
No, no, NO, no, no. I'm not cleaning up
another one of your messes. I'm not getting
involved. You figure this out.
                    (Starts to leave)
Mom is going to KILL you. Like literally,
KILL you.

                    EMILY
Alright, out. OUT.
                    (HANNAH leaves. EMILY is
                    alone. Lights change. Then,
                    to audience)
Nope, not yet. Right now we're at 3 minutes
and 42 seconds. Not even close.
                    (Lights back on)

                    EMILY
Ok, you can come out now. She's gone.

          (SAM enters from closet)

                    SAM
Sorry about leaving my calc book out.

                    EMILY
It's ok, she totally thought it was hers.

               (Silence)

                    SAM
Do you really like Nickelback?

                    EMILY
No, I don't.
                    (Beat)
Shut up.

                    SAM
I don't know if I can talk to you any
more....
                EMILY
Let it go, will you?

                    SAM
For a minute there I thought she was going
to find me.

                EMILY
How was it in there?

                    SAM
Not good.

                EMILY
It didn't bite you, did it?

                    SAM
No, I wrapped him up in a sweater.

                EMILY
Which sweater?

                    SAM
I don't know, blue, white stripes...

                EMILY
You idiot, that's Hannah's! She was so
uptight about letting me borrow it, she's
gonna kill me.

                    SAM
Sorry. I didn't know.

                    EMILY
This is a disaster. What on earth are we
going to do about this dumb squirrel?
                    (There is a bump in the
                    closet. Both scream. HANNAH
                    runs in)

                    HANNAH
Emily? You ok—
                    (Sees SAM)
Who are YOU?

                    SAM
Hi, I'm Sam. This isn't what it looks li--

                    HANNAH
                    (To EMILY)
You WERE hiding a boy in the closet!

                    EMILY
Technically yes. But--

                    HANNAH
You saucy little minx, you.

                    EMILY
Hannah, it's not like that.

                    HANNAH
I have to say I'm relieved. I mean, for a
minute there you had me convinced there was
a squirrel in there.

                    (EMILY and SAM look at each
                    other as there is another
                    bump in the closet)

HANNAH
Oh my god there is a squirrel in there.
Emily, what have you done?

EMILY
Everything I told you was true, I swear!
Except for when you asked why I didn't call
anyone. I did. I called Sam.

SAM
Hi.

HANNAH
Wait a minute, I know you. We have calculus
together. You're always late.

SAM
Yeah, we do. You always shout out the wrong
answer.

HANNAH
                (Stares for a second. Beat)
Yeah, that's fair.

EMILY
Hannah, if you're willing, I'd really
appreciate your help with this whole, uh,
situation.

HANNAH
Fine, okay, I'll help. What's the plan?

SAM
There isn't one.

                    HANNAH
Wonderful. I guess someone should go get
the thing and we can figure out what to do
with it from there.

                    EMILY
Okay.

                    HANNAH
Who's gonna do it?
                    (SAM and EMILY both touch
                    their noses, as in "nose
                    goes")

                    HANNAH
Oh, real mature, guys.

                    EMILY
You lost.

                    SAM
Have fun in there.

                    HANNAH
Hell no.
          (To EMILY)
You got us into this mess, you do it.

                    EMILY
Me? I can't.

                    HANNAH
You had no problem trying to mercilessly
kill it with my calc book.

                    SAM
Actually, it was my calc book...

                    EMILY
Whatever.

                    SAM
She has a point.

                    EMILY
I know I do. You're the guy.

                    SAM
So?

                    EMILY
Go. Get the squirrel. Be a man.

                    SAM
I find that highly offensive.

                    EMILY
Sam, not now...

                    SAM
Just because I'm of the male gender does
not mean my behaviors have to align with
the specific stereotypes of being a "man."

                    HANNAH
Wow. Okay. Fine, I'll do it.
                    (HANNAH walks over and opens
                    the closet)
Uh, guys? There isn't a squirrel in here.

                    SAM
Are you sure?

                    HANNAH
Uh, there's a mangled bloody sweater on the
floor, but—
                    (Realizes it's hers)

19

Emily! I told you if anything happened to that sweater...

> (Scene pauses. Lights
> change.)

            EMILY
8 minutes and 42 seconds...So far, I have lied to my sister, several times, and now, I ruined her sweater. She'll always be my sister. She'll always be there for me, but wow...I screwed up.
> (Lights up)
I know. I know.
> (Pause)
Sam did it.

            HANNAH
It's ok. It doesn't matter. It's just a sweater.
> (Piercing shriek comes from
> closet. Hannah looks
> inside.)
Oh GOD, it's hanging from the ceiling.

            EMILY
Shut it! Shut it! Shut it!
> (HANNAH shuts the closet door)

            SAM
Well, that didn't work.

            HANNAH
I got it.

            SAM
What?

            HANNAH

I know how we can get the squirrel.

                    SAM
Really? How?

                  HANNAH
Do you have a box somewhere?

                  EMILY
I think there's one under my bed. Why?

                  HANNAH
If it's on the ceiling, we can put it over
the squirrel and shake it to make it fall
in.

                    SAM
Interesting...

                  HANNAH
Then, once it's inside, we safely carry it
out.

                    SAM
That could work.

              (EMILY and SAM both touch
              their noses)

                  HANNAH
Damn.
              (Sighs)
Okay.

(HANNAH grabs box and goes
to closet. She completes the
task with squirrel squealing
and hissing. She hands the
box to EMILY.)

EMILY
(Exhales)
Wow.

HANNAH
Ya. It's really somethin'.

EMILY
Thanks for helping. I don't know what I'd
do without you.

HANNAH
(Laughs)
I don't know what you'd do either.
(HANNAH and EMILY hug)
This whole thing would have been pretty
funny, if you hadn't blatantly lied to my
face.

EMILY
I know--I'm sorry.

HANNAH
You're not. You didn't do a single thing to
help get rid of that squirrel. Not one
thing.

(Lights change)

                    EMILY
                (To audience)
I wish she was wrong. But she's not. I
single handedly got myself into this mess,
and I didn't lift a finger to get myself
out. That's messed up.
                (Lights back on)
You're right.

                    HANNAH
You'd better clean up because I'm sure as
hell not going to help you.
                (HANNAH exits)

                    EMILY
                (To Sam)
Thank you.

                    SAM
It's nothing.

                    EMILY
That's not true. I'm always dragging people
into my messes, and I just can't--

                    SAM
Is your life always like this?

                    EMILY
Like what?

                    SAM
Hectic? Otherworldly? Full of poor
decisions?

                    EMILY
Kind of.
               (Looks around)
Wow, what a mess. Where do we even start?

                    SAM
Wait, what?

                    EMILY
How are we going to clean this up? I could
use the help.

                    SAM
You think I'm going to clean all of this up
for you?

                    EMILY
Well I mean, I'd rather not have to deal
with this all by myself.

                    SAM
               (Stares)
I think I've done enough.
               (Turns to leave)

                    EMILY
Wow, just like that?

                    SAM
Honestly, Emily, what do you expect? This
is too much for me. I'm sorry, you're on
your own. I'm not going to get you out of
these messes anymore.
               (SAM exits)

                    EMILY
               (Sighs, looks around, sees
               box on the floor. She walks
               over, looks inside.)

Oh God.

(Lights change. EMILY speaks
to audience.)
Yep, I killed a squirrel, my sister hates
me, and my boyfriend won't even talk to me.
And now, I have to clean all of this up.
The cherry on top of a pretty horrible 15
minutes.
(Timer goes off)
There we go. Done.
(Pause)
But you know what? It's over. It literally
cannot get any worse.
(With dawning realization)
The next fifteen minutes will be better,
and the next fifteen, and the next...
(Pause)
My sister will forgive me, she's family
after all. And Sam? There are plenty of
other boys out there.
(With final understanding)
I guess my point is, in the end, none of
this really matters after all.

(END SCENE)

CLYDE'S CONSCIENCE

A 10-minute One Act Play
for
1M, 2F

By
Caroline Haroldson

Cast of Characters

Clyde: A sweet, nerdly
                                romantic who is
                                painfully aware of
                                his own social
                                awkwardness.

Sarah: A grounded and
                                smart young woman
                                Clyde's age.
                                Despite her past
                                history of being
                                unlucky in love,
                                she remains
                                confident yet
                                realistic about
                                relationships.

Conscience: A female
                                manifestation of
                                Clyde's inner
                                voice who nags,
                                belittles and
                                points out all of
                                Clyde's mis-steps.

Props needed: Bouquet of flowers.
Set requirements: Two chairs and a table.

Scene
A classy restaurant in Cleveland, Ohio.

Time
Present day. Evening.

28

AT RISE: Clyde sits at a table for two
with wilted flowers. Sarah, enters. She
sees Clyde sitting alone and approaches
him.

                    SARAH
Hi. Are you Clyde?

                    CLYDE
               (Too shy to speak)
I...I'm...

                    SARAH
I'm...Sarah?

                    CLYDE
Ah! Sarah! Right!

                    (Suddenly the stage goes
                    dark, CONSCIENCE enters,
                    rolling her eyes. The scene
                    freezes, except for Clyde.)

                  CONSCIENCE
Oh Clyde...Here we are on yet another date,
and what is the first thing you do?

                    CLYDE
I messed up already?

                  CONSCIENCE
YOU FORGOT HER NAME. Who goes on a blind
date and doesn't remember the girl's name?
You essentially blew it in less than 5
seconds. You've hit a new low, Clyde.

                    CLYDE
Okay, okay. I'll try harder. I promise.
Just...leave me alone for a bit, okay?

                  CONSCIENCE
Five. Minutes.

               (CONSCIENCE disappears. The
               scene recommences. SARAH
               begins looking at the menu.)

                    SARAH
Do you know what you're having?

                    CLYDE
Oh...No...I already ate.

               (CONSCIENCE reappears with a
               bewildered look on her
               face.)

                    SARAH
Oh...I guess I won't get anything then.

               (The scene freezes)

                  CONSCIENCE
Clyde.

                    CLYDE
WHAT?! I'm not hungry!

                  CONSCIENCE
Clyde!

                    CLYDE
She can eat if she wants to!

CONSCIENCE
Clyde!!

(The scene resumes)

CLYDE
If you're hungry, then eat. I'll just
watch.

SARAH
(Surprised)
You'll what?

CLYDE
Watch....you eat?
(Terrified look towards
CONSCIENCE, who glares at
him.)

SARAH
I'm going to have to give that a no.

CLYDE
You look nice.

SARAH
(Genuine)
Thank you.

CLYDE
Usually I don't like those kinds of dresses
(Pause)
But on you it's kind of cute.

SARAH
Only kind of?

31

                    CLYDE
              (Turns to CONSCIENCE)
Help.

                  CONSCIENCE
Clyde, you're unbelievable. Just relax.
Just act cool.

                    CLYDE
So...sports....

                  CONSCIENCE
Talk about something you know something
about, idiot.

                    CLYDE
So...science...

                    SARAH
Did you see that "Aliens" piece on
Discovery last night?

                    CLYDE
              (Genuinely interested)
You know I wanted to, but I didn't. How was
it?

                    SARAH
I didn't watch it either. I read on your
profile that you love Discovery channel, so
I figured maybe you had.

                    CLYDE
I put that down?
                  (To himself)
God, I AM a nerd.

                    CONSCIENCE
YA THINK?

                      SARAH
What?

                      CLYDE
Oh nothing. Did you know that humans most
likely developed from sea sponges?

                      SARAH
I didn't! That's very interesting.

                      CLYDE
Really?

                    CONSCIENCE
                 (As SARAH nods)
No.

                      CLYDE
                 (To CONSCIENCE)
I wasn't asking you!

                      SARAH
You weren't?

                      CLYDE
              (Snapping back to reality)
No, I was! I was talking to the...to
my...never mind. I must be making a
terrible impression.

                      SARAH
I dated a schizophrenic for 3 years.
Believe me, you're all
golden at this point.

                        33

                         CLYDE
No kidding!

                         SARAH
No! Seriously, he had these voices in his
head and he talked to them constantly. It
was sad, really.

                      CONSCIENCE
That's not you, Clyde. I'm just your inner
goddess. I'm actually the one keeping you
sane.

                         SARAH
He was so weird.
                   (Laughing)
He collected igneous rocks and would give
them pet names and stuff.

                      CONSCIENCE
Just pretend you don't have an igneous rock
collection. I always said it was weird.

                         CLYDE
Actually...I have a rock collection...
                (Glances at CONSCIENCE)
Metamorphic rocks, though.

                      CONSCIENCE
It doesn't matter what kind of rock is it,
you're still a capital N nerd!

                         SARAH
                  (Covering up)
Well that's...good...because the only thing
I really liked about him was his rock
collection.

CONSCIENCE
She's lying. She's so obviously lying.

SARAH
So...you come here often?

CONSCIENCE
No. Say no.

CLYDE
Yes.

CONSCIENCE
Why do I even bother with you...?

CLYDE
But I'm usually alone...because I've been
single for like, ever.

SARAH
(Laughing nervously)
Oh, that's funny...you're...funny....

(CLYDE is silent)

CONSCIENCE
(To CLYDE)
Laugh.
(CLYDE laughs loudly)
Not like that, like an actual human.
(CLYDE laughs normally but a
bit too long)
Okay, okay it wasn't that funny.

CLYDE
Oh, I almost forgot!
(Presents wilted flowers)
I got these for you!

35

CONSCIENCE
(Disgusted)
Those are the most-

SARAH
They're beautiful! Thank you.

CONSCIENCE
If she's a liar, she's a damn good one.

SARAH
Chrysanthemums. My favorite!

CONSCIENCE
(Slow clap)
We finally did something right, Clyde.

CLYDE
See? It's going well.

CONSCIENCE
I have to admit I'm impressed. Given the last few dates you've been on...Shall we review?

CLYDE
We shall NOT review. I'd rather forget about all t--

CONSCIENCE
There was that poor little soul you compared to a rare species found in the depths of the Amazon, do you remember her? Or that sweet girl from Romania who couldn't get through a sentence without you making a vampire joke. Or--

                    CLYDE
Please stop.

                    SARAH
Stop what?

                    CLYDE
Uhh...

                    CONSCIENCE
Quick, say something clever.

                    CLYDE
Please stop...being so...
                    (Dramatically)
beautiful.

                    CONSCIENCE
That's the best you could do?

                    SARAH
Hey Clyde?

                    CLYDE
Yeah?

                    SARAH
I need to say something.

                    CONSCIENCE
Oh god, she has herpes.

                    CLYDE
You have herpes?

                    SARAH
No. Honestly Clyde, I was really nervous
for tonight. I haven't dated since Lionel,
and that relationship wasn't exactly
healthy. I was scared that I wasn't ready
to date again, but what's great about you
is that now I don't feel so alone. I
understand why you're scared, and I get
that you're nervous. I am too. I just want
you to know that I don't think you're
crazy. It's okay to show your ugly side
a little sooner than expected. That's
better than showing it too late.

                  CONSCIENCE
She's the one, Clyde. Hold on to her and
never let go.

                    CLYDE
So, you don't think I'm weird?

                    SARAH
                  (Laughs)
Oh, you're definitely weird. But that's
fine with me. You don't have to try so
hard.

                  CONSCIENCE
You know what this means, Clyde.

                    CLYDE
                 (Confused)
What? What does it mean?

                  CONSCIENCE
I've got to take over, at least for now.

                    CLYDE
                 (Confused)
Why? She said--

                  CONSCIENCE
I'm your true self, Clyde. I'm the part of
you that makes you special, unique, and
honestly, I'm the reason you have friends
at all. Let me handle this.
                    (CONSCIENCE moves to take
                    CLYDE's place, but CLYDE
                    makes no move to leave.)
Don't you want to be happy?

                    CLYDE
                  (Sadly)
Okay.

                    (CLYDE grudgingly gets up
                    and CONSCIENCE takes his
                    place. He watches the scene
                    from behind the chair
                    CONSCIENCE is now sitting
                    in. CONSCIENCE speaks with
                    perfect first date poise and
                    charm.)

                  CONSCIENCE
So, what do you do?

                    SARAH
I'm a teacher. Fifth grade.

                  CONSCIENCE
How fascinating! How is that?

                    SARAH
It's great, it really is. I've learned so
much from these kids; It's inspiring to see
so much potential in human beings. They
inspire me every day, and taught me that
life is much too short to be self
conscious.
                    (CLYDE turns over his
                    shoulder to look back at
                    Sarah)

                    CLYDE
You know what? No.
                    (CLYDE makes a move to take
                    back his chair from
                    CONSCIENCE)

                    CONSCIENCE
Excuse me?

                    CLYDE
I really like this girl. How is putting up
all my walls going to help me with her?

                    CONSCIENCE
Face it, Clyde. You're embarrassing. You
have a rock collection. You watch the
Discovery Channel. You care way too much
about grammar...

                    CLYDE
Okay, maybe I do. I'm not perfect, but are
you honestly going to sit there and tell me
that she is? I'm willing to go out on a
limb here, and if you think for a second
that my self-consciousness is going to get
in the way of that, then you're crazy.

CONSCIENCE
You do realize that when you're insulting
me, you're insulting yourself...

CLYDE
I'm not going to change myself just because
you think I should.

CONSCIENCE
Fine. I'll just go then.
            (CONSCIENCE gets up, and
            heads for the door)
You're going to miss me.
            (CONSCIENCE exits)

CLYDE
Yeah, we'll see about that.
            (CLYDE sits down at table
            with newfound confidence)
Sarah, I like science.

SARAH
Was... that a secret?

CLYDE
I like science I have a rock collection and
I find Discovery Channel intellectually
stimulating. Often times I find myself
saying the wrong thing at the wrong time,
and I have the worst luck in the world.
Also, I will probably correct your grammar.
A lot.

SARAH
Clyde, I don't care about any of that.
Nobody's perfect.

41

                    CLYDE
                 (Relieved)
Yeah, you're right. Of course not.

                    SARAH
You won't have to worry about my grammar
though, I'm a teacher.

                    CLYDE
Oh, that's right. Fifth grade?
                 (SARAH nods)
I feel like that's such a good age for
kids, they're still young, yet they're so
close to maturation.

                    SARAH
You'd be surprised at how immature fifth
grade boys can be.

                         (They continue chatting
                         cheerfully, as CLYDE'S
                         CONSCIENCE reenters. She
                         looks at CLYDE, and smiles.
                         Her work here is done.)

                         (END SCENE)

<u>THESE SEATS ARE TAKEN</u>
(female cast)

A 10-minute One Act Play
for
2f

By
Caroline Haroldson

Cast of Characters

Isabella: A broody woman who
                              has come to the
                              movies alone in an
                              attempt to escape
                              her loneliness.

Anne: A woman of similar
                              age. Boisterous
                              and appearing to
                              lack any social
                              awareness.

Props needed: Bucket of popcorn.
Set requirements: Chairs.

Scene

A movie theatre, empty but for the two
characters. The theatre is slightly
darkened in anticipation of a film that
hasn't started yet. There are four rows of
about ten seats.

Time

Present day.

THESE SEATS ARE TAKEN
                    (female cast)

AT RISE: All seats are empty, save for the
back-middle seat, where ANNE sits.

                    ANNE
                    (ANNE drops her wallet. She
                    reaches under her seat to
                    get it just as ISABELLA
                    enters with a bucket of
                    popcorn. Upon hearing the
                    noise, ANNE drops all the
                    way down as ISABELLA takes
                    her seat in the first row.
                    The audience sees ANNE's
                    hands slowly grip the seat
                    in front of her as she pulls
                    herself up to grin at the
                    back of ISABELLA's head. She
                    suddenly, and very loudly,
                    speaks to ISABELLA)
   Well, looks like it's just the two of us!

                  ISABELLA
                  (Startled)
How long have you been back there?

                    ANNE
Since the last movie finished, about an
hour ago.

                  ISABELLA
I'm sorry, I didn't see you when I came in.

                    ANNE
I know. I was under the seat.

                    ISABELLA
                 (Understanding)
Ah.

                 (Realizing what she actually
                 said)
What?

                    ANNE
It's a funny story. I'll tell it. Well,
going to the movies is one of my favorite
ways to spend a day, besides finger-
painting and wood carving—

                    ISABELLA
I'm afraid I don't have the time for this.

                    ANNE
Sure you do!
                 (Looking up at the movie
                 screen)
It's not even previews yet.

                    ISABELLA
I happen to like the previews.

                    ANNE
You're lying.

                    ISABELLA
No I'm not.

                 (Pause. After a moment, ANNE
                 climbs over the seat in
                 front of her and sits down
                 next to ISABELLA.)

                    ANNE
Just what kind of person pretends to enjoy
previews?

THESE SEATS ARE TAKEN
(female cast)

                    ISABELLA
          (Looking straight ahead
          towards the screen)
The kind of person who likes to be left
alone.

                    ANNE
Fascinating.
          (ISABELLA doesn't respond)
Meaning you don't like to be bothered, or
you don't like any contact with other human
beings whatsoever?

                    ISABELLA
Both.

                    ANNE
I don't think that's healthy. Looks like
we'll have to get over that, now won't we?

                    ISABELLA
No, "We" won't.

                    ANNE
Well, we're going to try.

                    ISABELLA
"We're" not going to do anything.

                    ANNE
Aren't we?

                    ISABELLA
No, no we are not.

                    ANNE
Alright.
               (Beat)
I think we need to be more open-minded.

                  ISABELLA
That's enough. If you don't be quiet I'll
give you a piece of my mind.

                    (ISABELLA rises and begins
                    walking towards first row)

                    ANNE
In front of everyone?
                    (Referencing the empty
                    theatre)

                  ISABELLA
Oh jeez.

                    ANNE
Someone's grumpy.

                  ISABELLA
You're surprised?

                    ANNE
Well, there's no need to get all upset.

                  ISABELLA
I'm not upset. Just exhausted.

                    ANNE
Really? From what?

                  ISABELLA
Talking. To you.

                    ANNE
I'm touched.

                         ISABELLA
Don't be.
                    (Pause)

                         ANNE
I just realized I never told you my story.

                         ISABELLA
What story?

                         ANNE
The one about why I was under the seat.

                         ISABELLA
I don't want to hear it.

                         ANNE
Why not? It's a good story.

                         ISABELLA
If I listen to your story, will you promise
to leave me alone?

                         ANNE
Sure.

                         ISABELLA
You said it was a long story, how long
exactly?

                         ANNE
Four words.
                    (Counting on fingers)
I. Dropped. My. Wallet.

                    ISABELLA
And that required you to go all the way
under your seat?
                    (ANNE shrugs)
And stay there?
                    (ANNE smiles)

                    ISABELLA
Well. Alright. I'm going to watch the movie
now.

                    ANNE
But it hasn't started yet.

                    ISABELLA
Then I am going to sit here pretending to
watch the previews while you sit there, not
saying or doing anything.

                    ANNE
How about breathing?

                    ISABELLA
What about it?

                    ANNE
Can I breathe?

                    ISABELLA
Sure.
                    (ANNE gets up and walks
                    along the side of the
                    theatre as if to sit next to
                    ISABELLA)

                    ISABELLA
No, no, no, you are staying over there.

                    ANNE
Why? The view is better up here.

                    ISABELLA
               (Rises to change seats)
Then I'll sit back there.

                    ANNE
Good idea. Me too.

                    ISABELLA
               (Sits back down)
Then I'll sit up here.

                    ANNE
Excellent. Me as well.

                    ISABELLA
How about this; wherever you will be, I
will not. Be.

                    ANNE
What's your name?

                    ISABELLA
No.

                    ANNE
Interesting, is that short for something
else?

                    ISABELLA
I...what?

                    ANNE
Nora! Your name is Nora isn't it.

                    ISABELLA
It is not Nora, I just...don't want to tell
you.

                     ANNE
Ohh...insecure?

                    ISABELLA
No.

                     ANNE
My name is Annie, Anne for short.

                    ISABELLA
Anne for...short?

                     ANNE
Exactly. Think about it, ANNE is fewer
syllables when you say it right. "Annnnnn"

                    ISABELLA
                 (Thinking about it)
Annie...Annn...

                     ANNE
 See?

                    ISABELLA
That's stupid.

                     ANNE
It's not stupid. It's smart. Deal with it.
You never said your name.

                    ISABELLA
Isabella

                    ANNE
Oh!
                    (With completely sincerity)
What's that short for?

                    ISABELLA
It's not "short" for anything?

                    ANNE
What's it long for then?

                    ISABELLA
Long for?

                    ANNE
Izzie?

                    ISABELLA
No.

                    ANNE
Bella?

                    ISABELLA
No.

                    ANNE
Belle?

                    ISABELLA
Whatever.

                    ANNE
Why do you hate me?

                    ISABELLA
Because I can.

                    ANNE

53

That's a terrible reason.

                    ISABELLA
I don't care.

                    ANNE
You don't care?

                    ISABELLA
I really don't.

                    ANNE
Don't ever get married, Bells. Or have
children.

                    ISABELLA
               (Dripping sarcasm)
Well, just because you asked...

                    (The next section shouldn't
                    have the same playful sense
                    of the first section but
                    should still remain light.
                    Don't play into the
                    dramatics.)

                    ANNE
Can I ask you a question?

                    ISABELLA
No.

                    ANNE
Why are you here alone?

                    ISABELLA
                    (Pause)
What?

                    ISABELLA
Why isn't anyone with you?

                    ISABELLA
I could ask the same thing of you.

                    ANNE
                    (Chuckling)
I think you already know the answer to
that.

                    ISABELLA
I'm not sure, I guess I just prefer it.
                    (Beat)
Going to a movie by myself, I watch it with
my own pure, organic view. I don't react in
the same way as I would if I had someone
with me, I come out of it knowing exactly
what I thought.

                    ANNE
That sounds like a lie.

                    ISABELLA
It's not.

                    ANNE
No one prefers being alone. No one.
                    (Pause)
I don't have anyone to bring.
                    (Pause)

                    ISABELLA
No one?

                    ANNE

No one.

                    ISABELLA
Me neither.
                         (The lights to the theatre
                         dim as the movie begins.
                         ANNE and ISABELLA sit in
                         silence for several seconds,
                         when ISABELLA turns to ANNE
                         as if to say something, but
                         ANNE raises a finger to her
                         lips.)

                    ANNE
It's rude to talk during a movie. Don't you
have any manners?
                         (ISABELLA gives an
                         exasperated sigh and picks
                         up her popcorn from the
                         floor. ANNE helps herself to
                         a handful and ISABELLA
                         whisks the bucket away.
                         After a few seconds, she
                         relents and offers the
                         bucket to ANNE).

                    (END SCENE)

<u>THESE SEATS ARE TAKEN</u>
(male cast)

A 10-minute One Act Play
for
2m

By
Caroline Haroldson

Cast of Characters

Theodore:

A broody man who has come to the movies alone in an attempt to escape his loneliness.

Charles:

A man of similar age. Boisterous and appearing to lack any social awareness.

Props needed: Bucket of popcorn
Set requirements: Chairs

Scene

A movie theatre, empty but for the two characters. The theatre is slightly darkened in anticipation of a film that hasn't started yet. There are four rows of about ten seats.

Time

Present day.

THESE SEATS ARE TAKEN
(male cast)

AT RISE: All seats are empty, save for the
back-middle seat, where CHARLES sits.

                    CHARLES
               (Charles drops his wallet.
               He reaches under his seat to
               get it just as THEODORE
               enters with a bucket of
               popcorn. Upon hearing the
               noise, CHARLES drops all the
               way down as Theodore takes
               his seat in the first row.
               The audience sees Charles's
               hands slowly grip the seat
               in front of him as he pulls
               himself up to grin at the
               back of THEODORE's head.
               Suddenly and very loudly to
               THEODORE.)
Well, looks like it's just the two of us!

                    THEODORE
               (Startled)
How long have you been back there?

                    CHARLES
Since the last movie finished, about an
hour ago.

                    THEODORE
I'm sorry, I didn't see you when I came in.

                    CHARLES
I know. I was under the seat.

                    THEODORE
                (Understanding)
Ah.

                (Realizing what he actually
                said)
What?

                    CHARLES
It's a funny story. I'll tell it. Well,
going to the movies is one of my favorite
ways to spend a day, besides finger-
painting and wood carving—

                    THEODORE
I'm afraid I don't have the time for this.

                    CHARLES
Sure you do!
                    (Looking up at the movie
                    screen)
It's not even previews yet.

                    THEODORE
I happen to like the previews.

                    CHARLES
You're lying.

                    THEODORE
No I'm not.
                    (Pause. After a moment,
                    CHARLES climbs over the seat
                    in front and sits down next
                    to THEODORE.)

                    CHARLES
Just what kind of person pretends to enjoy
previews?

                    THEODORE
              (Looking straight ahead
              towards the screen)
The kind of person who likes to be left
alone.

                    CHARLES
Fascinating.
                    (THEODORE doesn't respond)
Meaning you don't like to be bothered, or
you don't like any contact with other human
beings whatsoever?

                    THEODORE
Both.

                    CHARLES
I don't think that's healthy. Looks like
we'll have to get over that, now won't we?

                    THEODORE
No, we won't.

                    CHARLES
Well, we're going to try.

                    THEODORE
We're not going to do anything.

                    CHARLES
Aren't we?

                    THEODORE
No, no we are not.

CHARLES

Alright.
(Beat)
I think we need to be more open-minded.

THEODORE

That's enough, if you don't be quiet I'll
give you a piece of my mind.
(THEODORE rises and begins
walking towards first row)

CHARLES

In front of everyone?
(Referencing the empty
theatre)

THEODORE

Oh jeez.

CHARLES

Someone's grumpy.

THEODORE

You're surprised?

CHARLES

Well, there's no need to get all upset.

THEODORE

I'm not upset. Just exhausted.

CHARLES

Really? From what?

THEODORE

Talking. To you.

CHARLES

I'm touched.

THEODORE
Don't be.
(Pause)

CHARLES
I just realized I never told you my story.

THEODORE
What story?

CHARLES
The one about why I was under the seat.

THEODORE
I don't want to hear it.

CHARLES
Why not? It's a good story.

THEODORE
If I listen to your story, will you promise
to leave me alone?

CHARLES
Sure.

THEODORE
You said it was a long story, how long
exactly?

CHARLES
Four words.
(Counting on fingers)
I. Dropped. My. Wallet.

THEODORE
And that required you to go all the way
under your seat?
(CHARLES shrugs)

THEODORE
And stay there?
(CHARLES smiles)

THEODORE
Well. Alright. I'm going to watch the movie
now.

CHARLES
But it hasn't started yet.

THEODORE
Then I am going to sit here pretending to
watch the previews while you sit there, not
saying or doing anything.

CHARLES
How about breathing?

THEODORE
What about it?

CHARLES
Can I breathe?

THEODORE
Sure.
(CHARLES gets up and walks
along the side of the
theatre as if to sit next to
THEODORE)

THEODORE
No, no, no, you are staying over there.

                    CHARLES
Why? The view is better up here.

                    THEODORE
                (Rises to change seats)
Then I'll sit back there.

                    CHARLES
Good idea. Me too.

                    THEODORE
                (Sits back down)
Then I'll sit up here.

                    CHARLES
Excellent. Me as well.

                    THEODORE
How about this; wherever you will be, I
will not. Be.

                    CHARLES
What's your name?

                    THEODORE
No.

                    CHARLES
Interesting, is that short for something
else?

                    THEODORE
I...what?

                    CHARLES
Norton! Your name is Norton isn't it.

                    THEODORE

65

It is not Norton, I just...don't want to tell you.

                    CHARLES
Ohh...insecure?

                    THEODORE
No.

                    CHARLES
My name is Charlie, Charles for short.

                    THEODORE
Charles for...short?

                    CHARLES
Exactly. Think about it, Charles is fewer syllables when you say it right. "Charlz"

                    THEODORE
                 (Thinking about it)
Charlie...Charlz...

                    CHARLES
See?

                    THEODORE
That's stupid.

                    CHARLES
It's not stupid. It's smart. Deal with it. You never said your name.

                    THEODORE
Theodore.

CHARLES

Oh!
(With completely sincerity)
What's that short for?

THEODORE

It's not "short" for anything?

CHARLES

What's it long for then?

THEODORE

Long for?

CHARLES

Theo?

THEODORE

No.

CHARLES

Teddy.

THEODORE

No.

CHARLES

Ted?

THEODORE

Whatever.

CHARLES

Why do you hate me?

THEODORE

Because I can.

CHARLES

67

That's a terrible reason.

                    THEODORE
I don't care.

                    CHARLES
You don't care?

                    THEODORE
I really don't.

                    CHARLES
Don't ever get married, Ted. Or have
children.

                    THEODORE
              (Dripping sarcasm)
Well, just because you asked...

                    (The next section shouldn't
                    have the same playful sense
                    of the first section but
                    should still remain light.
                    Don't play into the
                    dramatics.)

                    CHARLES
Can I ask you a question?

                    THEODORE
No.

                    CHARLES
Why are you here alone?

THEODORE
(Pause)
What?

THEODORE
Why isn't anyone with you?

THEODORE
I could ask the same thing of you.

CHARLES
(Chuckling)
I think you already know the answer to
that.

THEODORE
I'm not sure, I guess I just prefer it.
(Beat)
Going to a movie by myself, I watch it with
my own pure, organic view. I don't react in
the same way as I would if I had someone
with me, I come out of it knowing exactly
what I thought.

CHARLES
That sounds like a lie.

THEODORE
It's not.

CHARLES
No one prefers being alone. No one.
(Pause)
I don't have anyone to bring.

(Pause)

THEODORE
No one?

69

                    CHARLES
No one.

                    THEODORE
Me neither.
                    (The lights to the theatre
                    dim as the movie begins.
                    CHARLES and THEODORE sit in
                    silence for several seconds,
                    when THEODORE turns to
                    CHARLES as if to say
                    something, but CHARLES
                    raises a finger to his
                    lips.)

                    CHARLES
It's rude to talk during a movie. Don't you
have any manners?
                    (THEODORE gives an
                    exasperated sigh and picks
                    up his popcorn from the
                    floor. CHARLES helps himself
                    to a handful and THEODORE
                    whisks the bucket away.
                    After a few seconds, he
                    relents and offers the
                    bucket to CHARLES).

                    (END SCENE)

CHEAPER THAN THERAPY

A 10-minute One Act Play
1m and 1f
Or 2m, 2f

By

Caroline Haroldson

Cast of Characters*

David:

Jennifer's fiancé. An "Indoor" person who is uncomfortable in nature. A young adult who hasn't quite mastered communication skills or tact.

Jennifer:

A young woman David's age who prides herself on her independence and self-reliance, but sometimes confuses this with stubbornness.

* Names may be changed to suit the gender identity of the actors.

Props needed: An inexpensive, simple pup tent.

Scene

Remote woods. Very late afternoon.

Time

Present day.

AT RISE: JENNIFER and DAVID stand with packaged tent and backpacks at their feet. JENNIFER is holding the instructions for pitching the tent while DAVID looks over her shoulder.

                    JENNIFER
"Hello and thank you for selecting our brand for your use in any and all upcoming camping adventures. We are--"

                    DAVID
Just skip down to the directions.

                    JENNIFER
Your mother said to read the booklet word for word, cover to cover.

                    DAVID
No. She said the directions. Read the directions word for word, cover to cover.

                    JENNIFER
These are the directions.

                    DAVID
No, they're not. That's just the pointless beginning stuff.

                    JENNIFER
It says right here on the front, "Directions."

                    DAVID
Fine, go ahead. Read the whole thing.

JENNIFER
Alright. "Thank you for selecting our brand for your use in any and all upcoming camping adventures. We are positive you will be more than satisfied with our stress-free, easy to construct product. Be sure to read the instructions thoroughly and follow them in the order they are written for the best results." That means no skipping steps, David.

DAVID
Whatever.

JENNIFER
"We hope you enjoy putting together your tent. Happy camping!"

DAVID
Happy camping? It really says that?

JENNIFER
Yeah, right here.

DAVID
That's really dumb.

JENNIFER
(Under her breath)
This is dumb.

DAVID
What was that?

JENNIFER
This is FUN!

DAVID
Well I'm glad you think so.

74

          (Points to directions)
Could you hand me that, Jen?
          (JENNIFER hands over
          directions)
It's only three steps?

          JENNIFER
Yep. Three simple steps.

          DAVID
That doesn't seem quite right.

          JENNIFER
Well, that's what it says.

          DAVID
Right, because this definitely looks like a
three-step process.

          (They both look at
          directions, confused.)

          JENNIFER
I can't even tell what materials are
supposed to be used for what.

          DAVID
It's-it's like pictograms, I can't make
heads or tails—

          JENNIFER
Let's just gather everything together, and
then go from there.
          (They start grabbing
          materials and grouping them
          together as they talk.)

DAVID

You know, I'm glad we're doing this.

JENNIFER

Not like we had much of a choice.

DAVID

Well...

JENNIFER

Your parents kind of forced it on us.
                    (Beat)
But it's great. I think it's really
romantic of them to send us to this cliff's
edge, knowing I'm terrified of heights.
Somehow, I feel like that was your mother's
idea.

DAVID

It was! This is the exact spot they decided
to spend the rest of their lives together,
and come on, the view is pretty amazing.

JENNIFER

As long as we don't fall to our deaths
while sleeping.

DAVID

Don't worry. The tent gets hammered down
with stakes so it's completely safe.

JENNIFER

I wouldn't be too sure about that. I heard
about this one couple whose tent slid down
a mountainside and they just went down.

DAVID

Because they were stupid and didn't hammer
in the stakes to their tent.

(DAVID holds up stakes)
See, Stakes.

JENNIFER
(Not listening)
And there was another story about this
family who pitched their tent too close to
the river's edge, and it was swept away.
(Pause)
They didn't even find the bodies, or the
tent.

DAVID
Well, we are nowhere near a river.
(Puts his arms around
JENNIFER to comfort and
assure her)
....and we will stake our tent. Come on,
it'll be easy. I did this all the time as a
kid. This worked for my parents, they've
been married for almost 30 years, and it
worked for my brother and his wife Linda,
and they're...happy...

JENNIFER
I just don't get how putting up a tent can
be a factor in two people deciding if
they're ready to get married or not. I
mean, is anyone really ready?

DAVID
(Stops counting, looks
straight at JENNIFER)
Well I would hope so.

JENNIFER
David, that's not what I meant.

DAVID

77

Look, my parents said we didn't have their
blessing unless we pitched this tent
without calling off the engagement. Sure,
that sounds stupid, but I trust them, and
it means a lot to me to have their consent
on this. So if you could just try, Jen, for
me, I don't think that's too much to ask.

                    JENNIFER
               (Nods. Counts materials.)
Ok, we have two weird chain-y things, one
tent cover, and four stakes. I can't help
feeling like we forgot something.

                    DAVID
Nope, I double checked everything. See,
this is easy.
               (Grabs directions)

                    JENNIFER
Not so much.

                    DAVID
What?

                    JENNIFER
The directions show pictures of what the
tent is supposed to look like, it just
doesn't say how or why.

                    DAVID
Helpful.

                    JENNIFER
But what I think we're supposed to do is
put these
                    (Indicates support rods)
like this
                    (Crosses arms to form X)

DAVID
                    Uh-huh. That looks right.

                    JENNIFER
                    (Finds hole)
Here we go!
                    (Grabs rod and tries to push
                    it through. It's too small.)
Oh no.

                    DAVID
What's wrong?

                    JENNIFER
It doesn't fit.

                    DAVID
What do you mean it doesn't fit?

                    JENNIFER
I mean it doesn't fit, how much more
literal do you want me to be?

                    DAVID
Let me try.
                    (Tries. Fails.)
Either this tent is the most poorly made
piece of junk I've ever seen in my life or
we're doing something wrong.

JENNIFER
What could we possibly be doing wrong? It seems like pretty generic instructions.

DAVID
I don't know.

JENNIFER
Where is this tent even from?

DAVID
I don't know, my dad gave it to me before I left. It should say on the front.

JENNIFER
(Looking at label on tent packaging)
Brought to you by Dollar Tree?!

DAVID
Well. That explains it.

JENNIFER
Well we could widen the hole with something sharp. Did you bring your Swiss Army knife?

DAVID
No.

JENNIFER
So, our first date was an appropriate time to bring it, but going camping in the middle of the woods is not?

DAVID
I didn't think either of those decisions through.

                    JENNIFER
Wait a minute—

                    DAVID
What now?

                    JENNIFER
If we cut it, it will be too loose.

                    DAVID
What do we do?

                    JENNIFER
Well, what did you do the last time you
went camping?

                    DAVID
The last time I went camping?

                    JENNIFER
Yeah, didn't you do this "all the time" as
a kid?

                    DAVID
I mean...not all the time...

                    JENNIFER
But still a lot...right?

                    DAVID
Well...funny story.

                    JENNIFER
What do you mean?

DAVID
My part in helping the family pitch the tent was less...interactive.

JENNIFER
Interactive? What do you mean interactive?

DAVID
My job was to stand safely to the side and...read the directions out loud to the rest of my family.

JENNIFER
(Silence, then)
So you're telling me that when you were bragging nonstop about "All the camping experience" you have on the drive here, you were referring to your experience reading the directions??

DAVID
Well, now you're making it sound bad.

JENNIFER
Well, you know what? Since that's what you seem to do best, here.

(Throws directions at DAVID)

DAVID
Honestly?

JENNIFER
Reading directions seems to be all you that you are able to do, so why don't you make yourself useful.

DAVID

These don't have words.

JENNIFER

Is that my problem?

DAVID
(Pause)
Yes?

JENNIFER

Please, David, I'm trying to figure this out.
(Looping rods through tent)

DAVID

I just don't understand why you have to be so damn controlling all the damn time. My mother was right. You are a control freak.

JENNIFER
(Angry)
What?

DAVID

She said you were a control freak. And a psychopath.

JENNIFER

Really? Now is the perfect time to bring this up? You really want to do this right now? Because I can go.

DAVID

Oh, let's go. Let's do this.

                    JENNIFER
First off, you haven't lifted a finger to
do anything in your life.

                    DAVID
That's not true, I lift several fingers on
a daily basis.

                    JENNIFER
You can't even bring yourself to loop rods
through a tent cover because it's so
beneath you. So, what do you do? You make
me do it.

                    DAVID
Now you're just being rude.

                    JENNIFER
And maybe the reason your mother is so
quick to call me a control freak is because
she's the biggest control freak I know.

                    DAVID
Don't talk about my mom like that.

                    JENNIFER
And furthermore, I've done everything to
put this together while you just stand
there doing nothing.

                    DAVID
Ah yes, you've done all of this yourself.
I'm so proud.

                    JENNIFER
At least I'm trying. You told me to try, so
I'm trying.

DAVID

Congratulations.

JENNIFER

You know what? I think it might be best if you just stay over there for a while.

DAVID

Fine.

JENNIFER

Fine.

DAVID

Fine.

(Silence)

JENNIFER

You still have the instructions.

DAVID

So?

JENNIFER

So, I need them.

DAVID

Figure it out yourself.

JENNIFER

Honestly? This is how it's going to go?

DAVID

I mean, you've made it pretty clear that I'm useless so—

JENNIFER

That's not even close to what I said.

DAVID

That's exactly what you said.

                    JENNIFER
David, just give me the directions.

                    DAVID
No.

                    JENNIFER
David.

                    DAVID
No.

                    JENNIFER
David, just give it to me.

                         (They start in a tug of war
                         with the directions)

                    DAVID
I won't give them back until you apologize
for what you said.

                    JENNIFER
I'm not going to apologize.

                         (The directions rip in half)

                    DAVID
That is not my fault.

JENNIFER
It's ok, we can still read them.
                    (David picks up two ripped
                    pieces and rips them to
                    shreds)
Why did you do that?

DAVID
I do not know.

JENNIFER
Fine. I have no problem doing this on my
own.
                    (Begins setting up tent)
I really hope you're catching the metaphor
here, David.

DAVID
I am, but I'm also refusing to acknowledge
it because it's stupid.

JENNIFER
Is that really what you think?

DAVID
Yeah...no...maybe?

JENNIFER
I don't care if you think it's stupid. It's
still there and it makes you look dumb.

DAVID
I'm not dumb, and if that's the attitude
you're going to have you can sleep outside
on the ground.

                    JENNIFER
You wouldn't dare.

                     DAVID
Oh, I would.

                    JENNIFER
Fine then you can put this up yourself.

               (Pause)

                     DAVID
Eh, that's ok. It's all yours.

                    JENNIFER
Fine.

                     DAVID
Glad to hear it.

                    JENNIFER
Good.

                     DAVID
You know what, Jen?
               (Silence)
I do not appreciate the way you are
belittling my task as the reader of
instructions. I'll have you know that I was
extremely helpful in camping situations,
and I find it, quite frankly, rude that you
are referring to my efforts in such a
negative way. Having an individual present
to read the instructions is an important,
if not integral, part of any camping
endeavor. Now I believe that if we work
together and try to tackle this thing as a
unit, we'll make a lot more progress.

JENNIFER
Thank you, that's what I've been saying.

DAVID
But I don't think we can do that without an
apology from you. You have been rude, and
disrespectful, not only to me, but to my
entire family. I can't stand for that. So,
whenever you are ready, I will be by this
tree waiting for your apology.

JENNIFER
Really? I have to apologize?

DAVID
Yes.

JENNIFER
And what if I tell you that's not going to
happen.

DAVID
Well I guess...I guess I'd call off the
wedding.
                    (Jennifer says nothing and
                    keeps working on the tent)
Jennifer?

JENNIFER
Just let me do this.

DAVID
No, Jen, I'll help. I'm sorry. I'm being
stupid.

JENNIFER
I really would have appreciated this
attitude 5 minutes ago.

                    DAVID
Well I'm sorry I didn't fit into your
little time schedule—

                  JENNIFER
No really, because it's done.

                    DAVID
              (Pause, shift to positivity)
We did it!

                  JENNIFER

No...I did it.

                    DAVID
              (Helping her up)
Oh, come on, it was a team effort.

                  JENNIFER

No, it wasn't.

                    DAVID
I'm going to call my mom right now and tell
her. Thank you, Jen, you don't know how
much this means to me.

                  JENNIFER
Stop it.

                    DAVID
Come on, we had a couple of rough patches,
but the important thing is the tent is up
and we have my parents' blessing.

                  JENNIFER
David, stop.

DAVID

What's the matter?

JENNIFER

I did this by myself.

DAVID
            (Sarcastically refers to
            tent)
And isn't it magnificent.

JENNIFER
            (Ignoring sarcasm)
No. I did this by myself.

DAVID

Are you trying to start another argument?
Because I really don't want to do that
right now. It's over. We've finished.

JENNIFER

No David, I don't want another argument.
But if that's what needs to happen to
figure this out, so be it.

DAVID

Jen...

JENNIFER

No David, there's no getting out of this
one. We're going to face this head on.

DAVID

No way out you say??
            (Climbs into tent and zips
            self in)

> JENNIFER

Really??

> DAVID

I don't want to fight anymore.

> JENNIFER

You're not doing a great job of making that happen.

> DAVID

I'll stay in here as long as I have to.

> JENNIFER

You can't hide from me forever.

> DAVID

Yes, I can. We've put up the tent. It's over now.

> JENNIFER

No...no it's not.

> DAVID
> (Pops head out)

What?

> JENNIFER

Somehow, I thought that pitching this tent would make me feel more prepared, but it just made me more unsure of everything.

> DAVID

Prepared for what?
> (Silence)
Jennifer, do you not want to get married?

JENNIFER
I'm just...not ready. I know I should be,
but I just...
(Pause)
I put up the tent, but it didn't prove
anything. It gave me resolution, but not in
the way I expected. Your parents were
wrong. This doesn't prove a thing.

DAVID
(Climbing out)
Jen, I'm not ready either.

JENNIFER
You're not?

DAVID
No. Why do you think I insisted on agreeing
to this stupid camping trip in the first
place? I thought that passing a ridiculous
relationship test would somehow make it
easier. I'm terrified.

JENNIFER
Thank God.

(They hug)

DAVID
It's too late for us to head down tonight.
We should stay here and head down in the
morning.

(JENNIFER nods)

JENNIFER
Now all we have to do is hammer in these
stakes and we'll be all set.

                        DAVID
What did you just say?

                      JENNIFER
The stakes. Hammer them in like you said we
had to do so we don't roll down the cliff's
edge.

                        DAVID
Oh no.

                      JENNIFER
What.

                        DAVID
The hammer. We forgot a hammer.

                    (END SCENE)

f Join us on Facebook!

One Acts that Don't Suck
#oneactsthatdontsuck

NOTES

NOTES

NOTES

NOTES

NOTES